CatDog Catcher

Based on the TV series *CatDog*®
created by Peter Hannan as seen on Nickelodeon®

Editorial Consultants: Peter Hannan and Robert Lamoreaux
Additional assistance provided by the CatDog Production Team.

SIMON SPOTLIGHT
An imprint of Simon & Schuster Children's Publishing Division
1230 Avenue of the Americas, New York, New York 10020

Produced by Bumpy Slide Books
Designed by sheena needham • ess design and development
Manufactured in the United States of America

First Edition   10 9 8 7 6 5 4 3 2 1

Library of Congress Cataloging-in-Publication Data
Hutta, K. Emily
CatDog catcher / by K. Emily Hutta and Eliot Brown ;
illustrated by Emilie Kong. —1st Simon Spotlight ed.
p.   cm.   —(Ready-to-read. Level 2, Reading together)
Summary: Two heads prove to be better than one when CatDog,
an animal who is half cat, half dog, is captured and taken to the dog pound.
ISBN 0-689-83004-1 (pbk.)
[1. Cats Fiction. 2. Dogs Fiction.]   I. Brown, Eliot.
II. Kong, Emilie, ill.   III. CatDog (Television program).
IV. Title.   V. Series.
PZ7.H9655Cat 1999
[E]—dc21
99-24002
CIP

CatDog Catcher

by K. Emily Hutta and Eliot Brown
illustrated by Emilie Kong

Ready-to-Read

Simon Spotlight/Nickelodeon

Dog had a bad case of spring fever. "It's springtime! I wanna sniff, I wanna dig, I wanna run!" he panted. "What do you feel like doing first, Cat?"

"I feel like lying right here with the
sun on my belly," Cat answered. "This is
purr-fect!"

"I know something even better to do!"
Dog said. "Let's go mark some territory!"

"Ow! My body, my body!" Cat wailed.
"Stop, Dog, stop!" shouted Cat. "We're
on Greaser turf now!"

But it was too late. The Greasers had spotted them.

Just as Cliff, Shriek, and Lube caught up with CatDog—SWAT—an enormous net trapped them all!

"Leaping Lumbago!" cried Rancid Rabbit, the dogcatcher. "Four dogs for the price of one!"

"Make that three dumb dogs and one angry cat," Cat said.

"What, what, what?!?" Rancid Rabbit asked. He pulled Cat out of the net. "Get lost. I have no bones to pick with any cats today."

Cat was not happy. "Don't let it happen again," he said.

Then Rancid Rabbit emptied his net into the back of his truck. He sped off toward the city pound.

Dog kept his face hidden until the coast was clear. "Close call," he said. "Thanks, Cat."

Back at home, Dog tried to sit still. He sniffed the air. "Cat, do you smell spring in the air?" he asked. "I think I smell the scent of whitefish chub."

Cat's mouth started to water.
"White . . . fish . . . chub?" he replied.
His eyes were widening. "What are we
waiting for?"

CatDog raced over the hill and into town. Suddenly they spotted the dogcatcher's truck.

Cat pulled Dog behind a fence. "Over here! Quick!" Cat said. "We have to keep all four of our eyes wide open."

Dog stuck his head around the corner
to see if the coast was clear. SWAT!
Once again, CatDog was trapped in the
dogcatcher's net.

"Ah-ha!" Rancid Rabbit shouted.

Surprise! Rancid Rabbit couldn't believe his eyes. Cat was back in his net! He didn't know that Cat had switched places with Dog again.

"Well, well, well," Cat said.
"Rancid, I think you're a few carrots
shy of a bunch!"

"Yeah, you crazy rabbit guy!"
Dog exclaimed.

CatDog's cover was blown!

In no time at all, Dog was cooling
his paws in the POUND!

Cat was very upset. "This is just
terrific!" he complained.

"Sorry, Cat," said Dog.

Next, Cat called Randolph from a phone booth for help. Inside the cell, the Greasers surrounded Dog.

"Now you're gonna get it," Cliff said.

"Can't run now," Lube said. "Uh, at least not too far."

"Wait!" Shriek shouted. "Does anyone notice something different here?"

The other Greasers and Dog all shook their heads no.

"Cat's not here!" Shriek exclaimed.

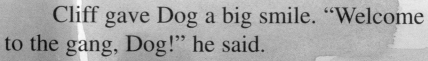

Cliff gave Dog a big smile. "Welcome to the gang, Dog!" he said.

Dog looked uncertain. "But what about Cat?" he asked.

"Forget about him," Shriek said.

"Yeah," said Cliff. "Us jaildogs gotta stick together."

"Uh, okay," agreed Dog.

Cat was still on the phone. "Okay, Randolph. You sure you can pull this off?"

"No problem," replied Randolph. "It'll be a piece of cake!"

Back in the cell, Cliff told Dog the Greasers' plan. "We're bustin' out. And since you are new to our gang, you have to dig our escape tunnel."

Dog didn't know what to say. "Thanks, guys. I won't let you down."

"You'd better not!" replied Cliff. "Here's your spoon. Now, dig!"

Dog worked hard at digging. Dog also worked hard at eating. The worms and dirt looked too good to resist.

While Dog stuffed his face, Cat decided to take action. Cat slipped into Dog's cell.

"Hiya, Cat," said Dog. "Where have you been?"

"I've been trying to get us out of here," said Cat.

Just then Randolph came down the hall. "I am from the law firm of Hairball, Hairball, Kitty, and Litter," he told Rancid Rabbit. "My client says that you are a cat burglar!"

"Your client?" Rancid Rabbit asked. He turned and saw Cat inside the cell.

Randolph explained: "My client is a cat. Not a dog!"

"Huh?" said Rancid Rabbit.

"This is a DOG pound," said Randolph. "You have jailed a CatDog. Half of this animal shouldn't be here at all. You must release them both at once!"

"Hey! What about us?" Cliff shouted.
"We're your jailhouse buddies, Dog!"

"I'm not a jailhouse dog anymore,"
replied Dog.

"This ain't the end," Cliff called.
"You're going to get it. Just wait until
we get out of here!"

Back at home, Dog asked: "What do you feel like doing now?"

"I'm happy right here," Cat said.

"Wanna go mark some territory?" asked Dog.

"This is our territory," replied Cat.

And that's exactly where they both wanted to be.